# BEETHOVEN
## LIVES UPSTAIRS

# BEETHOVEN LIVES UPSTAIRS

*Barbara Nichol*

ILLUSTRATED BY
*Scott Cameron*

SCHOLASTIC INC.
NEW YORK TORONTO LONDON AUCKLAND SYDNEY

30053000074495

No part of this publication may be reproduced in whole or in part, or stored in a retrieval system, or transmitted in any form or by any means, electronic, mechanical, photocopying, recording, or otherwise, without written permission of the publisher. For information regarding permission, write to Orchard Books, 95 Madison Avenue, New York, NY 10016.

ISBN 0-590-50830-X

Text copyright © 1993 by Classical Productions for Children Limited.
Illustrations copyright © 1993 by Scott Cameron.
All rights reserved. Published by Scholastic Inc., 555 Broadway, New York, NY 10012, by arrangement with Orchard Books.

12 11 10 9 8 7 6 5 4 3                5 6 7 8 9/9 0/0

Printed in the U.S.A.                08

First Scholastic printing, September 1995

For Jessica, Benjamin, and Sarah Eisen,
and for Elizabeth and Jonathan Milroy,
with all the love in the world

— B. N.


To my parents, Jim and Terry Cameron

— S. C.

On Thursday, March 29, 1827, the people of Vienna flooded into the streets. They came to pay their respects to Ludwig van Beethoven, the great composer, who had died three days earlier.

At three o'clock in the afternoon nine priests blessed the coffin, and the funeral procession left Mr. Beethoven's house for the church. So dense were the crowds that the one-block journey took an hour and a half.

I wasn't in Vienna on that famous day. I was a student of music in Salzburg at the time. But if you had looked carefully, you might have spotted in the crowd a little boy with a serious face. He is Christoph, my nephew, and there was a time when he came to know Mr. Beethoven quite well.

It was not a happy time in Christoph's life. He was only ten years old, and his father had recently died.

The first of Christoph's letters arrived at my door in the autumn of 1822. I was surprised that he had written. I had not seen my nephew for some years. . . .

7 September 1822

Dear Uncle,

I hope you will remember me. It is Christoph, your nephew, who writes. As to the reasons, I will not keep you in suspense. I write, Uncle, because something terrible has happened. A madman has moved into our house.

Do you remember that when Father died, Mother decided to rent out his office upstairs? Well, she has done it, and Ludwig van Beethoven has moved in.

Every morning at dawn Mr. Beethoven begins to make his dreadful noise upstairs. Loud poundings and howlings come through the floor. They are like the sounds of an injured beast. All morning Mr. Beethoven carries on this way. After lunch he storms into the street. He comes home, sometimes long after the house is quiet for the night, tracking mud and stamping his way up the stairs above our heads.

Mother says I mustn't blame him. He's deaf and can't hear the noise he makes. But he wakes up the twins, and they start their crying. They cry all day.

Uncle, I must make this one request. I beg you to tell my mother to send Mr. Beethoven away.

Your nephew,
Christoph

10 October 1822

My dear Christoph,

I arrived home last night to find your letter on the table in the hall. Do I remember you? Of course I do!

I should tell you that I have received a letter from your mother as well. As you know, she is concerned about you and wants you to be happy. She assures me that Mr. Beethoven is peculiar perhaps, but certainly not mad.

Christoph, Mr. Beethoven will settle in soon, I'm sure. I know that life will be more peaceful before long.

Your uncle,

Karl

*Having answered my nephew's letter, I left Salzburg for some weeks on matters related to my studies. In truth, I expected no further messages. The three letters that follow arrived in my absence.*

22 October 1822

Dear Uncle,

I hope you will forgive my troubling you, but I am sure that you will want to hear this news. Our family is now the laughingstock of Vienna.

I opened the door this morning to find a crowd in front of our house. They were looking up at Mr. Beethoven's window and laughing, so I looked up too. There was Mr. Beethoven, staring at a sheet of music. And Uncle, he had no clothes on at all! It was a dreadful sight!

You should see him setting out for the afternoon. He hums to himself. He growls out tunes. He waves his arms. His pockets bulge with papers and pencils. On the street the children run and call him names.

Mr. Beethoven is so famous that sometimes people stop outside our house, hoping they will see him. But if anyone asks, I say he has moved away.

Your nephew,
Christoph

29 October 1822

Dear Uncle,

I have now seen with my own eyes that Mr. Beethoven is mad. I will tell you the story in the hope that you will do something at last.

Last night, when I was getting ready for bed, I happened to look up. There were beads of water collecting on the ceiling above my head.

As usual, Mother was busy with the twins, so I climbed the stairs and crept along the hall to Mr. Beethoven's room. I looked in. He was standing there with no shirt on. He had a jug of water in his hands. He was pouring the water over his head, right there in the middle of the room, and all this time stamping his feet like he was marching or listening to a song.

You should see my father's study! Do you remember how tidy he was? Well, now there are papers lying everywhere — on the floor, on the chairs, on the bed that isn't made. There are dirty dishes stacked up and clothing crumpled on the floor. And another thing, he has been writing on the wall with a pencil!

I said nothing to Mr. Beethoven, of course. Luckily, he did not see me, and I ran back down the stairs.

Uncle, if you are thinking of coming to our aid, there could be no better time than now.

Christoph

5 November 1822

Dear Uncle,

Another week has passed, but life is no calmer here.

I've been thinking. If Mr. Beethoven were to leave, surely we could find someone nice to live upstairs. The rooms are large, and Father's patients always talked about the view of the river. Father used to carry me down to the riverbank on his shoulders, even down the steep part right behind the house.

I think that of all the places in the house, I like the outside best. I can be alone there and get away from all the noise inside. But on this day even the stray dog outside was making his pitiful voice heard.

Yours truly,
Christoph

22 November 1822

My dear Christoph,

Today I have returned home from a visit away to find three of your letters waiting. Christoph, I will admit that Mr. Beethoven does not seem to be an easy guest.

Perhaps I can help, though, by saying that as strange as Mr. Beethoven seems, there are reasons for the way he acts.

They say he is working on a symphony. And so, all day long, he is hearing his music in his head. He doesn't think, perhaps, how very strange he sometimes seems to us.

Tomorrow I am leaving Salzburg again and traveling with friends to Bonn, the city where Mr. Beethoven was born. I know I will find something to tell you about and I will be sure to write on my return.

Uncle Karl

10 December 1822

Dear Uncle,

It has now been a full three months since Mr. Beethoven moved in, but our household has not yet become like any sort of ordinary place.

Mr. Beethoven has a friend named Mr. Schindler who visits almost every day. He always says, "Poor Mr. Beethoven. He is a lonely man."

You know that Mr. Beethoven is deaf. When he has visitors, they write what they want to say in a book. He reads their message and answers them out loud. He has a low and fuzzy voice.

Mr. Beethoven's eyes are weak as well. When he works too long by candlelight, his eyes begin to ache. He sometimes sits alone, with a cloth wrapped around his head to keep out the light. He sits, not seeing and not hearing, in his chair.

Uncle, there is no hour of the day when I forget that Mr. Beethoven is in the house.

Your nephew,
Christoph

*I returned to Salzburg in late January of 1823.*

22 January 1823

Dear Christoph,

I have this very day returned from the place where Mr. Beethoven was born. It seems his family is well remembered there.

They say Mr. Beethoven's grandfather was a musician, in charge of all the music at the palace. And Mr. Beethoven's father was a musician, too. But Christoph, this father was an unhappy man who took to drink. Mr. Beethoven was not a happy child.

People who lived near their house remember hearing music coming from the attic late at night. Sometimes Mr. Beethoven's father would come home long after dark and get the young boy out of bed. He would make him practice his piano until dawn.

The little Beethoven would play all night, tired and cold, his face awash with tears. Finally, as the sun came up, he would go to bed to the sound of morning bells.

I will send this letter right away, in the hope that you will answer soon.

Affectionately,

Uncle

4 February 1823

Dear Uncle,

This afternoon a messenger arrived, bearing a note for
Mr. Beethoven.

The messenger said to me, "This is from Prince Karl
Lichnowsky. But the prince says that if Mr. Beethoven's door is
closed, he is not to be disturbed."

Mr. Beethoven must be a terrible man if even a prince is
afraid of him.

Your nephew,
Christoph

15 February 1823

Dear Christoph,

I've been thinking of your story about the prince. Christoph, I don't think the prince is afraid of Mr. Beethoven. I believe he is showing him respect. In Vienna, music is so loved that even a prince will tread carefully around a composer.

Alas, Mr. Beethoven has not returned their kindness. He has not been gentle with the fine people of Vienna, and they have done everything they can to please him. Mr. Beethoven has always had rough manners. He turns down their invitations, dresses carelessly to visit, and arrives late for their dinners.

Sometimes he is very angry if he is asked to play his music. There is one famous story of a grand lady who got down on her knees one evening to beg Mr. Beethoven to play. He refused.

And there is another tale about a prince who teased Mr. Beethoven for not playing at dinner. Mr. Beethoven flew into a rage. "There are many princes," he said, "but there is only one Beethoven."

My belief, Christoph, is that a prince has more to fear from Mr. Beethoven than has a little boy.

Affectionately,

Uncle

26 February 1823

Dear Uncle,

No news today but this — do you remember I once told you about a stray dog who was whining on the street? He is a small and spotted dog, and I have found a way to make him stop his crying.

Today he seemed quite pleased to share my sugar cake from lunch.

Christoph

2 March 1823

Dear Christoph,

I write again so soon because I have been making inquiries on your behalf.

I spoke today with a man who once worked for Mr. Beethoven, copying out music for the players. He told me that Mr. Beethoven never stays in one home very long. He moves often — as often as three times a year.

Sometimes Mr. Beethoven wants a sunnier home, sometimes shadier. Sometimes he says he cannot live on the ground floor; then he cannot live on the top. And I hear he has been asked to leave from time to time as well.

He has a restless nature, so perhaps before too long you will have your wish and quieter people will be living upstairs.

But in the meantime, tell me . . . is it true, as I have also heard, that Mr. Beethoven has three pianos in his room?

Your uncle

10 March 1823

Dear Uncle,

No, it is not true that Mr. Beethoven has three pianos. He has four! And you should see them! To begin with, some of his pianos have no legs. He takes the legs off to move them and so that he can play them when he is sitting on the floor. That way he can feel his playing through the floorboards, which he must do because, of course, he cannot hear.

But it's surprising that his pianos can be played at all. Many of the strings are broken and curled up. They look like birds' nests made of wire. And the pianos are stained inside from the times he's knocked the inkwell with his sleeve.

And Mr. Beethoven has all sorts of bells on his desk, and four ear trumpets to help him hear, and something called a metronome as well. It's a little box with a stick on it. The stick goes back and forth and back and forth and tells musicians how fast they should play.

Mr. Beethoven has a name for me. He calls me "the little gatekeeper" because I am always sitting outside on the step.

Yours truly,
Christoph
Gatekeeper

2 April 1823

Dear Christoph,

Your letter about Mr. Beethoven's piano has reminded me that there was a time when Mr. Beethoven was more famous for his playing than his composing.

When Mr. Beethoven first lived in Vienna, he would sit down with orchestras to play his music, without a single note written out. It was all in his head.

And the music he played! His music was so beautiful that sometimes people who were listening would start to cry. But Mr. Beethoven would laugh at them and say, "Composers do not cry. Composers are made of fire."

Now that Mr. Beethoven is deaf, of course, he plays the piano with the bumps and crashes you hear upstairs all day.

And I have another story for you, a story people tell about his deafness. One afternoon Mr. Beethoven was out walking in the woods with a friend. A shepherd was playing a flute nearby. Mr. Beethoven's friend said, "Listen!" and stopped to hear the flute. But Mr. Beethoven heard nothing. And so he knew, that day, that he was going deaf.

When Mr. Beethoven was still a young man, he began to hear humming and buzzing in his ears. At first he couldn't hear high notes. Then he couldn't hear soft voices. How frightening it must have been for him, Christoph, and how alone that man who lives upstairs must feel.

To hear Mr. Beethoven's story convinces me that I am the most fortunate man alive.

Your uncle

21 April 1823

Dear Uncle,

Do you remember my telling you that Mr. Beethoven leaves each afternoon for a walk? Did you wonder where he goes? Well, now I know, and I will tell you the story.

Mother sometimes says that instead of just staying on the front steps it would be nice if I'd spend some time inside. I used to believe she meant it until this morning.

I thought of something to play with the twins. I rolled up a bit of cardboard like an ear trumpet and put one end in little Teresa's ear. I said, "GOOD MORNING, BABY!" very loudly, and she started to scream. Mother said it hurt her. So I went outside again and sat in my usual place on the step.

Then Mr. Schindler came downstairs. He said to me, "The master needs new pencils," and off I went to the shop.

When I came back, Mr. Schindler was gone. No one was upstairs but Mr. Beethoven, and he was writing at his desk. I stamped my feet on the floor to get his attention and when he didn't notice I stamped harder until at last I was stamping as hard as I could. Then suddenly he turned around and saw me. When he laughs, he sounds like a lion.

So today I went along with him on his walk. At times Mr. Beethoven forgot that I was with him. He would hum and sometimes wave his arms. He took out his papers and made some little notes.

We walked outside Vienna into the tall woods and then past the woods and into the fields. Uncle, if you were to come to visit me, I would show you where we walked today.

Christoph

30 June 1823

Dear Uncle,

Spring has come and gone, and now it is summer. The house is quiet because tonight Mr. Beethoven has gone to Baden, where he will spend the hottest months. He will finish his symphony and then he will come back.

Tonight as I write you it is evening, but I cannot sleep with the sun still shining through the shutters. From my room I can hear Mother playing piano as she used to when I was small.

I have been sitting here thinking about something Mr. Schindler said. He said, "Mr. Beethoven works so hard because he believes that music can change the world."

*In the autumn of 1823 Mr. Beethoven returned to*
*Vienna from his summer lodgings.*

29 October 1823

Dear Uncle,

Mr. Beethoven has come home, and so our house is in an uproar again. Someone has given him another piano, and there was a lot of trouble getting it up the stairs.

And then last night he had a party. A lot of people went in and out very late, and the more cheerful they became upstairs, the noisier it was for us.

Finally, it was impossible to sleep. I could hear two ladies singing. I had seen them earlier, laughing on the stairs. They are called sopranos because they are singers who can sing very high.

Mr. Beethoven has a housekeeper. She says that when the sopranos come up the stairs, Mr. Beethoven rushes like a schoolboy to change his coat. And he won't let her make the coffee for them. It must be perfect, with exactly sixty beans for every cup. He counts them himself.

Uncle, I have asked Mother if you can come to visit. She said she would be delighted if you would. She thinks you would enjoy the goings-on.

Christoph

4 January 1824

Dear Christoph,

How glad I was to receive your letter. I hope you will forgive my very late reply. Did you know that your mother has written to me as well? She tells me there's a steady stream of great musicians up and down your stairs.

Since Mr. Beethoven is writing his Ninth Symphony in your very house, perhaps you will be interested in the things I have heard. According to the stories, Mr. Beethoven has felt that he is not appreciated in Vienna. He almost agreed to perform his new symphony in Berlin! I'm happy to say, though, that so many people begged Mr. Beethoven to change his mind that, luckily, he did.

And there is other news: they say the orchestra members are complaining about their parts. The bass players say their instruments aren't nimble enough for Mr. Beethoven's quick notes. The sopranos say their notes are just too high. All over Vienna the musicians are struggling with their tasks. His symphony will put to music the poem "Ode to Joy."

I hear as well that because Mr. Beethoven is deaf, he will lead the orchestra with another conductor — one who can hear — conducting alongside him.

Amid these great events, little gatekeeper, how is life at home? Do your twin sisters still torment you with their terrible shouts? Perhaps before too long I shall hear them for myself.

Uncle Karl

27 March 1824

Dear Uncle,

I know this will come as a surprise, but this time I write you with good news.

I was standing on the upstairs landing today when my favorite soprano came by to get tickets for the concert. At least she is now my favorite.

She had something to ask of Mr. Beethoven and she wrote her request in his book. Then she wrote another request, handed him the book, and winked at me.

He read her words and said, "Certainly. The boy and his mother will have tickets as well."

And so Mother and I will be going to the Ninth Symphony. I wrote "thank you" as neatly as I could in his book.

As for the twins, Uncle, of course they still torment me. It is what they were put on earth to do.

Now I have a new name for my sisters. I call them "the sopranos." It makes my mother laugh.

Yours truly,
Christoph

20 April 1824

Dear Uncle,

I know now that all of us have been quite happy of late.
And the way I know it is that in the past few days our happiness
has vanished once again. With the symphony just two weeks
away, Mr. Beethoven's moods are fierce.

Caroline, his housekeeper, is going to leave to marry the
baker next door. She told Mr. Beethoven today, and he became
very angry. He picked up an egg and threw it at her.

Then Mr. Schindler came rushing down the stairs like a
scalded cat. He had told Mr. Beethoven that his new coat won't
be ready for the concert in time. He tried to talk to Mr.
Beethoven about another coat but, as Mr. Schindler said, "The
master is in no mood for details."

And I have not helped matters. Today, when I was in his
room, I disturbed some of his papers as I was passing by his
desk. They fluttered to the floor. I am afraid these papers had
been ordered in some very special way because Mr. Beethoven
said, "Now I must do work again that I have already done."

Uncle, just when life was getting better, I have ruined
things again.

Your nephew

28 April 1824

My dearest Christoph,

How shall I console you? Perhaps by telling you that Mr. Beethoven is famous for his temper and that his moods are not your fault.

Imagine how frustrating his life must be. Imagine how lonely to hear no voices. Imagine hearing no birds sing, no wind in the trees, no pealing of bells. Imagine: he hears no music played, not even his own!

So Mr. Beethoven has a great temper. How could he not? But if you listen to his music, you will hear that his heart is great as well, too great to be angry for long at an innocent boy.

You write me that, for the moment, your happiness has vanished. I can give you my promise, Christoph, that unhappiness has a way of vanishing as well.

Your uncle and friend,

Karl

*The unsigned and undated note below was written in May of 1824,*
*on the eve of the first performance of the Ninth Symphony.*
*It arrived tucked into the letter that follows it.*

Dear Uncle,

    Mr. Beethoven has forgotten the incident with the papers. He squeezed my shoulder in a friendly way when he passed me in the hall this afternoon.

    Now the house is quiet, and I am alone. The concert is tomorrow night, and so, of course, I cannot sleep. I think of Mr. Beethoven alone upstairs. I have not heard him stir for quite some time. I wonder what he's thinking about. I wonder if he's awake tonight like me.

    Perhaps he is hearing something beautiful in his head.

7 May 1824

Dear Uncle,

Tonight I have been to the Ninth Symphony. It is very late. I have already tried to sleep, but it seems I cannot do so before I describe this night to you.

The concert looked as I expected. There was Mr. Beethoven on the stage, waving his arms as I have seen him do so many times upstairs. And there were the singers. I had seen them often too, tramping up and down our halls. And there were the musicians scowling at their charts. These sights were so familiar.

It was the music, Uncle, that took me by surprise.

And when the music ended, the audience was on its feet. Everyone was standing and cheering and clapping and waving scarves and crying and trying to make Mr. Beethoven hear them.

But he couldn't hear us and he didn't know that we were cheering until one of the sopranos took his sleeve and turned him to face the crowd. Four times the audience finished their clapping and then began to clap and cheer again. Up on the stage Mr. Beethoven bowed and bowed.

As the carriage took us home, I could hear the music in my head. But my thoughts kept turning back to Mr. Beethoven himself.

He has so many troubles, how can he have a heart so full of joy?

I cannot describe the music, Uncle. I can only tell you what the music made me think.

Uncle, how difficult Mr. Beethoven's life must be. To feel so much inside, even so much joy, must be almost more than he can bear.

Christoph

*In June of 1824 I finally paid a visit to Vienna, to the home of my sister, her twin girls, and Christoph. It was Christoph, of course, who took the most delight in explaining the many eccentricities of the genius up the stairs. This letter, the final portion of which is now missing, is the last in which my nephew mentions Mr. Beethoven. It arrived at my home in Salzburg almost a year after my visit to Vienna.*

31 March 1825

Dear Uncle,

As you know, Mr. Beethoven moved away soon after your visit. But I have seen him again and thought you might like to hear about it.

It was on the street. I saw him rushing by, humming to himself as always. I ran up and caught him by the sleeve. He looked confused at first, but then he recognized me. He said, "It's the little gatekeeper," and took my hands in his.

I took his book and asked if he was well. He had hoped his health would be better living away from the river. He told me his health has not improved. I wrote in his book that when I grow up I'm going to be a doctor like my father and then I will make him better.

He asked about Mother and the twins, and he was glad to hear that Mother is teaching piano again. And then I told him that we miss him. He squeezed my hands and looked down at the ground.

And as for other news, the twins have finally stopped their screaming. I know, however, that our good luck will not hold. I have seen them exchanging looks in their carriage and can see that they are hatching some new plan.

But Uncle! Best of all! Mother has agreed to let me keep the spotted dog.

I have named him Metronome, because of his wagging tail.